KAPPIYA'S STORY COLLECTIONS -2

VIKRAMADHITHYA AND VETALA

KAPPIYA CLASSICS

Contents

Foreword

KAPPIYA CLASSICS

Hello Dear Readers

I am Tamizhiniya Tamizhdesan

when I was studying in school my teachers used to conduct lessons between many good books and that conduct gave me confidence that I can conduct more than a hundred topics with introductory speech. My Technical education helped a lot in this aspect. When I became a teacher I assisted my students in the way our teachers guided us.

My school, college and workplace friends lives scattered in different countries like the poem of Eelam Poet V.I.S. Jayapalan, the families of them too scattered in different nation, whereas I live in the Land of my Mother Language(Tamilnadu). Among my friends who are running to strive for their living, I have selected the publishing department to read their lives and pass it on to others. We are publishing legendary works under Kappiya Vasipagam. So far we have published more than 1500 books in package type.

I have used the library a lot in my school, college and work life. Novelist Vasu Murugavel writes that he brought a bundle of books from a person, read them and returned them. Similarly, I have imported hundreds of books read them and sent them back. I have also written novel in Tamil and English, also a book based on the Culture of Tamil People.

My son Imayakappiyan (8) started learning his Tamil lettering from the texts of our cover pages. The same way he is gaining the knowledge of book names, authors also the technical knowledge in publishing and helps us in many ways. My husband Tamizhdesan guides me about the packaging materials of the book contents and his creative thinking of book cover page makes me to create some unique cover pages. We three feel very happy to be in this field which makes us to learn continuously.

I take great pleasure in publishing many of the war stories I have been reading. Movements that fight for the people are viewed by populists as scumbags. An example of this is the Tiger movement, which was not only similar to a government but also created various departments and the personality within them. There is no doubt that writing and reading them as well will diversify you.

FOREWORD

-Tamizhiniya TamizhDesan

ONE

1. Bhoja Raja gets Vikramadhithya's throne

There was a great king called Bhoja in the city of Ujjaini. The city was near a big forest. Lots of wild animals used to come from the forest in to the city and trouble the people. So Bhoja decided to hunt for those wild animals and destroy them. One day he started in the early morning with large number of hunters and other assistants to the forest. They hunted and destroyed lots of wild animals. By noon, they were all very tired and far away from the town. They then started searching for some water, food and a place to take rest. Suddenly they saw a field of sweet corn. There was big well with water also in it. In the middle of the field, its owner called Saravana Bhatta, was standing on a platform and guarding the field from animals and birds. As soon as he saw them, he told them "Oh king, a hearty welcome to you along with your soldiers. Please take as much corn as you want and also use the water of the well. You can all take rest in the garden afterwards." The king was very happy and he along with the army entered the garden and started eating the sweet juicy corn. At this time Saravana Bhatta got down from the platform. Suddenly he started shouting at them, "Hey cruel king, I am a poor man, some how living with the yield of this corn. If you all start eating the corn, how will I live? Also the water in the well would be taken by you all. Then how will I water my corn plants tomorrow. Go away immediately." Taken aback, Bhoja said sorry and asked his people to go away from the field. While they were withdrawing, Saravana Bhatta again climbed on the platform. Suddenly he started talking to them, "Oh great king, why are going away. You must be very hungry. Please take as much corn you want and also drink, as much water you want."

Then king Bhoja realized that Saravana Bhatta was completely changing, once he climbs on the platform. He called Saravana Bhatta and told him,

"Dear Brahmin, I want to buy this corn field. I would give you ten times its price. "Saravana Bhatta happily accepted the price, gave the land to the king and went away. The king asked his army to dig at the spot, where the platform was there .After some time they found there a majestic golden throne with 32 golden steps. On each step , there was a golden doll. King Bhoja became extremely happy and wanted to take the throne to his palace. But in spite of great efforts, they were not able to move the throne even a little bit from that place. Then he called his wise minister and asked him, "Dear Sir, Why am I not able to move this throne to my palace? The minister replied, "Sir, It looks that this throne belonged to a great king. This has been here for a very long time. So you have to worship to the throne before moving it." The king sent for his priests and a proper worship was done to the throne. Then they were able to move it. They then got the throne cleaned and placed it in the chamber of the king. The king wanted to sit on the throne and rule his country. On a good day, after again worshipping the throne, he started climbing it. As soon a he started climbing it, all the thirty two dolls on the throne, clapped their hands and started laughing. The king asked the first doll, "Why are you laughing?"

The doll replied, "King Bhoja, this throne belonged to King Vikramadhithya, You are too small a man compared to Vikramadithya. He was a great valorous, just and efficient king, who was interested in the welfare of his people, we feel that you are not fit to climb the throne."

King Bhoja asked the first doll, "Who was this king Vikramadithya. I would like to know more about him. Then only I can tell you, whether I am as good as a king as he was."

The first doll then the story of "Who was Vikramadhithya?"

2. Who was Vikramadhithya?

Once upon a time, there was a very learned man called Samudhra Guptha. He learned all the Vedas and all that is known to all the teachers of India. He was not satisfied. He felt that there must be some thing more, which I have not learned. So he was wandering all over India in search of teacher who knew more than him. One day he reached a forest near Ujjain. He was tired. So he took bath in a river in the forest and slept in the shade of a big Banyan tree. On the top of the Banyan tree there lived a ghost (Brahma Rakshas). Seeing Samudhra Guptha, the ghost was terribly attracted. It then woke up Samudhra Guptha and asked him, "Brahmin, who are you. Why have you come to this dense forest? On the other shore of the river, there is the town of Ujjain. If you go there you will get food and also proper resting place." Samudhra Guptha replied. "I do not know who you are? My name is Samudhra Guptha. I am in search of a teacher who knows more than me and learn from all that he knows. Till I meet such a person, I am not interested in food or rest."

The ghost replied, "Samudhra Guptha, I know much, much more than you. I am willing to teach you all that I know. It would take six months night and day, for me to teach. But during these six months, you should neither take food nor sleep. I would give you the power not to take food and also not get sleep. But once I finish my teaching and you leave this forest, you would be as hungry as you have not taken food for six months and you will get sleep as if you have not slept for six months. If it is agreeable to you, I will immediately start the lessons." Samudhra Guptha agreed to this. The ghost wrote each lesson on the leaf of the Banyan tree and dropped it down. As soon as he learned one lesson, the next lesson was given. In six months time Samudhra Guptha had learned all that the ghost knew. He thanked the ghost and started towards Ujjain.

But as soon as he crossed the forest, he became a bundle of mere bones covered by a skin and started sleeping as if he has never slept. One lady called Alangara valli who passed by the way saw him. She took him to her home. When the doctor came he told, "This man has not eaten any food for six months. Neither has he slept for six months. If you want to save him, cook lot of rice. Then keep on massaging his body with the cooked rice. If you do it like this for three months, he would wake up." Alangara valli agreed and kept on massaging Samudhra Guptha with cooked rice. After three months, Samudhra Guptha woke up. Then he asked," Where m I? I want to go to my home." Alangara valli then told him all that happened and requested Samudhra Guptha to marry him." Samudhra Guptha was not willing. Then Alangara valli complained about Samudhra Guptha to the king. The King after hearing the story of Samudhra Guptha wanted him to marry his daughter also. His minister as well as the king's priest wanted him to marry their daughters also. Samudhra Guptha married all the four ladies. The priests daughter became mother too a son called Vara Ruchi, the kings daughter became mother to a son called Vikramadithya, the minister's daughter became mother to a son called Bhatti and Alangara Valli became mother to a son called Bharthruhari.

The king gave his kingdom to Samudhra Guptha and left to the forest

.Samudhra Guptha ruled over the country in a very nice manner. After all his children were well grown up, Samudhra Guptha became sick and was about to die. He was seen crying by his sons. Then Bharthruhari who was the eldest son asked him, "Father, why are you crying?" Samudhra Guptha replied, "Being the eldest, you will become king after me. But since you mother is a low caste woman, if you get children, I would surely go to hell." Bharthruhari then told his father, "Father do not worry at all. I may marry but I will see to it that, I never have any children." Samudhra Guptha died a happy man.

Bharthuhari the king

Bharthruhari married one thousand queens and was ruling the country in a great manner. Among them he was particular fond of a very pretty Ananga Sena.During this time one Brahmin did great austerity (thapas) to please Goddess earth. At last , pleased with his devotion, she came in person and asked him, "Oh Brahmin, I am greatly pleased with your devotion. What can I do for you?"
The Brahmin replied , "goddess , I am worried that I am getting old and weak. I want you to make me young always and forever,."
Goddess earth gave him a golden pomegranate fruit and told him, "By eating this you would be young forever" and disappeared.. Then the Brahmin thought, " I am extremely poor. What is the use of my remaining young forever. Instead of eating this, I would make a present of this fruit to the great king Bhatruhari." He did like that. The king was pleased and gave him lot of wealth and comforts.
But the king did not want to eat the fruit himself. He thought, it would be great if his queen Ananga Sena was young forever. He called and gave her the golden pomegranate. But the queen had a secret lover- The driver of the kings Chariots. She gave it to him. That driver had another lover. She was the maid servant who was cleaning the horse stables of the king,. He gave it to her. That lady kept the fruit in the top of her basket and was returning home. The king who was passing that way identified the divine fruit.He got dejected with life and decided to become a saint. So he made his younger brother Vikramadhithya , the king and another younger brother Bhatti as his Prime minister.

How Vikramadhithya built his capital

Vikramadhithya was a very intelligent and valorous king. Bhatti was very cunning and wise. They ruled the country well. After some time Vikramadhithya wanted to build a new capital city. So whenever they got time, Vikramadhithya and Bhatti went on searching for a good place to establish their capital city. One day they came across a very suitable spot in a place called Vachana giri. There was a beautiful river called Gunavathi flowing by its side. There was also a temple for Goddess Kali in the adjoining forest. When Bhatti went inside the forest and examining it,, he saw an inscription on a stone in the temple. It was written. " There is a big Banyan tree near the temple pond. There are seven hanging shelves made of rope on the tree. In the middle of the pond , there is a big and sharp spear. Suppose a man can cut off , all the seven rope shelves in one cut and fall head first on the spear in the pond, The goddess of this temple would bless him." He then told Vikramdhithya to climb on the tree, hold on to one shelf, keep his feet on the opposite shelf and rotate. By doing this the rope holding all the shelves would become joined. Then with his sword he can cut the rope and fall on the Spear in the pond, head first. Vikrama agreed . He did as instructed by Bhatti . But when he was about to be killed by the spear, Goddess Kali herself came and saved him. He blessed him as follows." You would build your capital city , in this place with the treasure buried in this city and call it Ujjain. You would become a great king and become the emperor of all India" . Vikramadhithya Buily a new city in Ujjain and became a great king.

How Vikramadhithya got the throne?

When this was going on, Devendra the king of heavens had a problem. He had several dancers in his court. Of them Rambha and Urvasi were the best. But they were jealous of each other. Since both of them were equally pretty and equally adept in dancing, King Devendra could not decide as to who should be made the Chief Dander of his court.His minister suggested , "Sir, There is a great and intelligent king in Ujjain called Vikramadhithya. Possibly he can help you in taking the decision". Devendra then sent his chariot to Ujjain. At that time , it was evening and Vikramadhithya was alone. He immediately accepted the invitation of devendra and came back to Heaven, in the chariot sent by Devendra,

First day he made Ramba and Urvasi dance. He was not able to see any difference.He told them ,"I will see you both dance once more tomorrow and then take the decision." .He welt to his lodgings and made two flower Bouquets. Within each bouquet , he put some stinging bees , in both the flower bouquets. Next day he requested Ramba and Urvasi to do a fast dance , keeping the flower bouquet in their hand. When they danced after some time, the dance movements became very viguorous. At that time Ramba sghirieked with pain , because the bees in the bouquet, Vikramadhithya stopped the dance competition and told Devendra, "Sir Uravasi is a better dancer , because she was having stylish and soft movement of her limbs and did not hurt the bees. Ramba , though a good dancer, lost her tender movements when she was dancing vigourously."

DEvendra became happy and presented him with a gem studded throne with 32 steps. Each step was being protected by a divine doll. He blessed him to rule over India sitting on the throne for another 1000 years.Vikramadhithya was greatly pleased and came back along with the throne.

Country six months and forest six months.

When he called and narrated all this to Bhatti he asked him, "That is fine. But I will die early and not live for one thousand years. " Vikramadhithya became sad on hearing this.Bhatti said that he would find out some method to live for one thousand years. That night Bhatti went to the Kali temple. When he went Goddess Kali had gone out for a walk outside the temple. He waited for her. Goddess Kali returned at mid night. She was surprised on seeing Bhatti and asked him, "Bhatti why have you come here sat this time?" Bhatti replied, "goddess, I want to live for one thousand years.Kali told him, "I can give you the boon provided , you bring me the cut head of Vikramadhithya. " Bhatti immediately agreed and went inside the palace. And woke up Vikramadhithya. He told him, Brother, I want your cut head urgently." Vikramadhithya agreed. Bhatti cut the head of Vikramadhithya and took it to the Kali Temple. The goddess was pleased, and told him , "You will live up to 200 years." As soon as he heard the boon , Bhatti startedlaughing and told the Goddess, "My brother got the boon to live for one thousand years only a week back and now he is dead. I do not really know when I will die?" Goddess got angry and told him, "do not equate me with Devendra. Both you and your brother will live for 2000 years. " and she gave life back to vikramadhithya.

The brothers now had a problem. Both of themn would live for 200 years but Vikramadhithya would be king for only one thousand years. Bhatti found out a solution, Vikramadhithya would rule the country for six months (country six months) and the he wouls spent the next six months in the forest (forest six months). It was a great idea and they both ruled India for two thousand years.

Then the doll asked Bhija, "king, do you think you are as great as Vikramadhithya?"

By that time , it was evening and Bhoja went to his palace.

3. *Vikramadhithya and Vetala I*

On the second day king Bhoja again worshipped the throne and tried to climb the steps. Then the doll in the second step started laughing and King Bhoja asked the doll, why it was laughing.Then that doll said, "Are you as valorous as Vikramadhithya to occupy this throne?' King Bhoja replied, "I do not know much about Vikramadhithya. Can you tell some thing about him?" Then the second doll whose name was Madanabhisheka valli started telling:-

In times of yore, when Vikramadhithya was ruling this country, two miles away from the town of Ujjaini, there used to be a Kali temple. Near the temple was a cremation ground. In that cremation ground, there was a drumstick tree. In that drum stick tree, a corpse was hanging upside down. Inside, the corpse was a great Vetala (ghoul).Any body who controls the Vetala could almost attain anything he wants.

Near by an evil sage called Gnanaseela was trying be very powerful. He went on meditating in the Kali temple. Kali, being pleased came in front of him and asked, "Oh sage, what do you want?', Then the sage replied, "Devi, I want all the wealth of this world and want to be the most powerful man of the world." Kali replied "For getting that you have to do a great fire sacrifice and offer the heads of thousand kings. You also have to control, the Vetala of the drumstick tree."

The sage immediately started the fire sacrifice. He could easily catch hold of 999 kings, cut off their head and put it in the fire. He wanted to sacrifice the head of Vikramadhithya next. So he started going to the court of Vikramadhithya. Daily he would present the king, a pomegranate fruit. King without bothering about it, asked is minister to store it. One day the minister had gone away. The pomegranate fruit was in the king's chamber. The pet monkey of the king, broke open, the fruit. From inside the fruit red gems started falling. Then the king examined all the fruits given by the sage. All the fruits had invaluable gems in side them. So when the sage came next day, Vikramadhithya asked him, "Oh sage, why are you giving me such invaluable presents? What can I do for you? The sage replied, "King, I am giving the fruits because I like you. I have only one request. I live in the nearby Kali temple. Tomorrow at mid night, you should come alone there." The king agreed. The next day, king Vikramadhithya went o to the temple. When he went there, the devils and ghosts were dancing in the temple. Because Vikramadhithya was bold, he did not bother about them. The sage who was in the temple asked Vikramadhithya, "Dear king, I want a help from you. Near this temple, there is a cremation ground. In that ground, there is a drum stick tree. On the drum stick tree, a corpse would be hanging upside down. Please go and get it for me." Vikramadhithya did not even wait for a moment and went to the cremation ground and approached the drumstick tree. He took his sword and cut off the corpse from the tree. Though he heard sound of it falling, it went back to the tree again. Now he climbed the tree, untied the corpse and holding it tightly started walking towards the Kali temple. Then the Vetala inside the corpse started speaking, "King, I am a powerful Vetala. If you are going to carry me, there is a condition. On the way, I would tell you a story. At the end of the story, I would ask you a question. If you know the answer and do not tell it, then your head will break in to thousand pieces. But if you tell the correct answer, I would escape from you and start hanging in the drum stick tree again." Vikramadhithya agreed to this condition. The Vetala started telling its first story.

I The story of the just king.
There was a great king called Vichara, He had only one son. The prince one day went for hunting in the forest riding a horse. He chased animals deep in the forest. He was feeling very thirsty. He went in search of a pond. At last he found it. He saw a sage sitting there. The prince told the sage, "I am the prince of this country. I want to drink water in the pond. Please hold this horse till I come back." Then the sage told, "do you think, I am your servant? I cannot hold the horse for you? "The prince got very angry and beat the sage with his whip. The sage was wounded and went and complained to the king against the prince. The king immediately ordered the minister, to cut off the hand of the prince. When the minister told that it was not necessary, the king told, "The prince has behaved very harshly with the sage. What he has not done is not proper. Please cut off his hand."
The sage who was listening to all this pleaded with the king to excuse the prince. The king agreed with him and excused the prince.
The Vetala asked, "who is greater-the king or the Vetala?"

Vikramadhithya replied, "Ofcourse, the king, because he wanted to punish the prince, in spite f him being his only son."

The Vetala immediately went back to the cremation ground and started hanging upside down on the drumstick tree.

Second story of Vetala

There was a Brahmin called Agni swami. . He had a very pretty daughter called Mandarawathi. When she attained marriageable age, three very eligible Brahmin boys sought her hand. Each of them claimed that they are deeply in love with her and would die, if they are not able to marry her. As fate would have it, Mandaravathi, became sick and died. Her body was cremated. One of the Brahmin boys built a hut in the cremation ground and stayed there. Another of the Brahmin boys collected her bones and went on a pilgrimage to dip them in all sacred waters of India, The third became a sage and started travelling all over India.

One day the sage was partaking in a feast offered by a Brahmin. When he was eating food, the baby child of the Brahmin started crying. His mother got very angry with the child and threw the baby in a raging fire. The baby was burnt to ashes. The Brahmin sage refused to eat the food served to him. Then the baby's father chanted a Manthra and sprinkled water on the ashes of the baby. The child woke up as if he was sleeping. The Brahmin sage learnt that Manthra and returned back to the village of Mandarawathi. At the same time, the Brahmin who had gone on pilgrimage also returned with the bones. Then the bones were kept on the ashes and the Brahmin sage chanted the Manthra. Mandharavathi became alive again. All the three Brahmin boys claimed that she should marry them. The Vetala asked, Oh Vikramadhithya, whom should Mandarawathi marry?"

Vikramadhithya replied, "The man who guarded her ashes would marry her. This is because, the Brahmin sage by giving her life, became like her father and the man who carried her bones had the role of her son."

As soon as Vetala heard this, it freed itself and again to the Drum Stick tree and started hanging there.

Third story of Vetala.

There was a poor Brahmin. He had three sons. They were connoisseurs from birth. Their father wanted to do a yaga. For performing the yaga, they needed to bring a tortoise from the sea.

The first son said, "I will not touch this tortoise because I am a connoisseur for food. If I touch the tortoise, I will never be able to eat food again."

The second son said, "I am a Connoisseur of woman and my sensibility would be affected, if I touch the tortoise."

The third son said, "I am the connoisseur of sleep. If I touch this tortoise, I will never be able to sleep."

Since they were not able to reach any agreement, the three sons went and approached the king for judgment.

The king wanted to test them. He first took them and asked his servants, to serve the food prepared for him. While the second and third son enjoyed it, the first one refused to eat it saying, "That the rice prepared had the scent of a corpse." the king was aghast. But when enquiries were made, they came to know that the rice indeed was grown in a land which was once upon a time a cremation ground."

Then the king chose one of best ladies from his harem and sent her to be with the second son. But the second son told, "Take her away or I will die. A goat's smell is coming from her."

Again the king made enquiries and found that that girl grew up by consuming goat's milk.

That night a special bed was prepared for the third son. Twenty softest beds of the kingdom were arranged one on the top of the other. Over them ten softest bed sheets were spread. But after spending one night, the third son complained that the bed was a little rough in one place. When they examined it, they found that between the first and second bed, there was a hair of the lady."

Vetala asked, "That king was not able to judge who was the real expert, Can you?"

Vikramadhithya replied, "It is obvious. The first and second so were awake and their senses were sharp when they made the judgment. But in case of the third son he was sleeping. So the greatest expert is the third son.

Immediately the Vetala disengaged itself and went to the Drum stick tree,

Fourth story of Vetala

Vikramadhithya again went to the drum stick and caught hold of the Vetala. Along with it he started walking to the Saint's place. Then the Vetala told the following story.

In the southern country there was a wise Brahmin who was the minister to the king. He had a very intelligent son and a very pretty and intelligent daughter. The name of the daughter was Swayamprabha,

When Swayamprabha grew up , she told that she will marry a man who is either an expert in science, or a valorous hero or a very wise man. Her parents and her brother agreed to these conditions.

Once the Brahmin minister had to travel to a different country. There one Brahmin boy called Sastri approached him and sought the hand of Swayamprabha. The Brahmin told her condition. Then Sastri told that he was an expert of science. To prove this he constructed a plane which was flying in the sky. The Brahmin was happy and agreed to celebrate the marriage next Monday. Sastri brought the Brahmin in his plane to the southern country.

Meanwhile a Brahmin called Soora approached the brother of Swayamprabha and sought her hand. Her brother told the condition. Then Soora claimed he was valorous hero. He fought bare handed with a lion and killed it to prove his point. Then Swayamprabha's brother promised her in marriage to Soora, the next Monday.

While this was going on a Brahmin called Rishi approached Swayamprabha's mother and requested the hand of Swayamprabha. Her mother told about the condition. Then Rishi proved to her that he knew the past, present and future. So the mother promised to celebrate the marriage next Monday.

On Monday Sastri, Soora and Rishi reached the marriage hall. But by that time Swayamprabha had vanishes. Rishi by his powers found out that she was taken away by a fierce Rakshasa who was staying in a forest one thousand kilometers away. Sastri built a fast moving plane full of weapons. Sastri, Soora and Rishi travelled to the forest. There Soora fought with valour and killed the Rakshasa . They then brought back Swayamprabha to her home.

Now Rishi told that Swayamprabha was his because , without him they would not know where to search. Sastri claimed her as his because without him they could not have gone there. Soora claimed her, because without him, they could not kill the Rakshasa.

Now Vetala asked, "Oh king, to whom should Swayamprabha be given?"

The king replied, "Of course to Soora. For love belongs to valour and it is the duty of science and knowledge to serve valour.

The Vetala then freed itself and again started hanging on the drum stick tree.

Fifth story of the Vetala.

Again Vikramadhithya caught hold of the Vetala from the Drumstick tree and started walking towards the house of the sage. The Vetala told its fifth story

There was a young man called Rama in a great city. He was very handsome and a great devotee of Durga. One day when he was travelling on business, he saw a very pretty girl called Janaki. He immediately fell in love with her. Nearby was a temple of Durga. He entered the temple and told the Goddess, "Oh divine Goddess, I am in love with Janaki and want to marry her. Please help me do it. If you help me , next time when I come to this temple, I will sacrifice myself before you."

After this he enquired about Janaki and found out her whereabouts. When he returned back home he was very sad and listless. His father asked him, :"Rama what is the matter? After the last trip, you are very sad." Then Rama told him about his love to Janaki. Immediately Rama's father contacted Janaki's father and the marriage was arranged. It took place almost immediately. Rama and Janaki lived a very happy life. Janaki had a brother called Krishna. One day Krishna came to Rama's house and invited Rama and Janaki for a festival in their village. Rama accepted the invitation and accompanied Krishna. On their way was the Durga temple. Rama got the chariot stopped and went inside the temple . As soon as he saw Goddess Durga, he remembered his earlier promise. So he took the sword of the goddess and cut off his own head. When he was not coming out, Krishna came to enquire. When he saw that Rama had cut off his head, he also cut off his head. After some time Janaki came in. Seeing both her husband and brother dead, she also decided to sacrifice herself. When she took the sword, Goddess Durga appeared before her and told, "Janaki , I am so much happy with your devotion to your husband and brother. Please join their heads to their bodies., they will become alive. "

Janaki thanked the Goddess and did what she was told. But in the hurry she did a mistake. She joined Rama's head to Krishna's body and Krishna's head to Rama's body."

Vetala asked, Hey king who should be the husband of Janaki? "

Vikrama replied, "It should be the person having Rama's head. This is because it is the brain that dictates the actions wishes of a person."

Vetala immediately disengaged itself and went back to the Drumstick tree.

Sixth story of the Vetala:-

Again Vikramadhithya caught hold of the Vetala from the Drumstick tree and started walking towards the house of the sage. The Vetala told its sixth story.

In the city of Patna there was a king called Vikrama. He had a parrot as a pet. This parrot was a very wise one and gave him proper counsel, whenever he needed it.

According to its advice he married Princess Chandra of the Magadha kingdom. She had a talking Myna as a pet. This bird was also extremely wise. After the marriage the parrot and Myna were kept in the same cage .One day after being attracted by the Myna, the parrot requested her to marry him. Then the Myna told, "All males are very bad people. So I do not want to marry." Then the parrot told , "What you say is not true. On the contrary all, females are cruel people,."

They started fighting with each other and there was a lot of noise. Then after lot of arguments they decided to leave the matter to king Vikrama.

First Myna told the king , "All men are cruel"

The king asked "How do you say that?"

Then the Myna started reciting the following story:-

There was a rich merchant who had a son called Dhanadhatha. Dhanadhatha was a spend thrift and a man of loose morals. He used to drink , gamble and spend the money for unnecessary things. , Due to this he lost all his wealth. So he decided for going to some other country , where no body will know about him. He reached a city of Chandanapura and met a rich merchant. That merchant was impressed by the personality of Dhanadhatha and gave his daughter in marriage to him. That merchant gave lot of dowry and also gave very large quantity of ornaments to his daughter .Dhanadhatha then told his father in law that he needs to go to his place along with his wife. On the way he told his wife. "Travelling with so many ornaments is risky. Please remove them and hand it over to me. " she did it. After travelling some more time , he pushed her in to a well and vanished with all her ornaments. The merchant's daughter was saved by another way farer and returned home. She did not tell the truth to her father. She told her father that they were attacked by a gang of thieves, who removed all her ornaments and have taken away Dhanadhatha as a slave. The merchant became sad but consoled his daughter.. Dhanadhatha after spending all the money , again came back to the merchant o ask for more money. But the merchant's daughter saw him first and took him back to her home. That night Dhanadhatha killed his wife and stole all her new ornaments and ran away. "Oh king", asked the Myna, "does this not prove that all men are cruel."

Then the parrot to prove his point started telling another story.
There was a very rich lady called Vasudatha. Her father gave her in marriage to another rich man called Samudhra Datha of the neighboring country. Samudhra Datha loved Vasudatha very much and gave her , what all she wanted. Once she wanted to visit her father. He sent her to her home as he was busy with his work. In her home town Vasudatha saw a very strong and pretty man. She wanted to make love to him. So they reached an agreement. After some time Samudhra Datha came to take her wife away. That night , after he was asleep Vasudatha , went outside to meet her lover. She was wearing lot of ornaments. One thief who had come to her house to steal her ornaments followed her. When she reached the spot where her lover had promised to meet her., Vasudatha found that her lover had died. But a Vetala which had entered his body , made his limbs move. Thinking that her lover was alive, Vasudatha embraced him. Then the Vetala made her lover open his mouth and bite away the nose of Vasudatha. Vasudatha ran back home. The thief also followed her. After reaching there, she started shouting that her husband had bitten her nose off. The husband was produced before the king who sentenced him to death. The thief then went to the king and told, "Sir Samudhra Datha is innocent. This girl has a secret lover and his body is lying in the garden. You can see her nose in his mouth." The king sent some people and found that the thief was telling the truth. Samudhra Datha was released and Vasudatha was sentenced to death.
The parrot asked , "Oh king Vikrama, does this not prove that all women are cruel?"
The Vetala then asked Vikramadhithya, "Who is correct-the parrot or the

Myna?"

Vikramadhithya replied, "The parrot is correct. The cruelty of a wife to her husband is baser than the cruelty of the husband to his wife."

Vetala immediately disengaged itself and went back to the Drumstick tree.

Seventh story of the Vetala:-

Again Vikramadhithya caught hold of the Vetala from the Drumstick tree and started walking towards the house of the sage. The Vetala told its seventh story.

There was a great King. One day a hero called Veera entered his kingdom along with his wife named Dharma, Son named Surya and a daughter named kavya. He was holding in his hand a sword and a shield. He went and directly met the king and told him, "Sir, I would like to become the security guarding you. I am a great hero. But I need five hundred rupees per day as my salary."

The king was impressed and agreed. Veera was offered the job of guarding the king. The king felt that the compensation he was giving to Veera was very high. He sent his spies to enquire about it. They came and told him that out of the five hundred rupees, One hundred rupees was given to his wife to run his household. He would spend another one hundred to for buying articles of cleanliness and cloth. Another one hundred was given to the temple and rest of the money (two hundred) was spent on poor people.

The king was extremely happy with Veera. Then the rainy season started. There were torrential rains. Veera would stand in the rain and guard the king. As and when he wakes up , the king would check up whether Veera was doing his duty. One day when he woke up , he heard the wailing of a woman. He asked Veera to go and investigate as to why the lady was crying. Veera walked in the torrential rain towards the source of that wail .The curious king also followed. After some distance Veera met the woman who was wailing, he asked her."Mother, who are you and why are you wailing?"

The lady replied, "I am the mother earth. I know that the good king of this country is going to die in three days. I am sad because of that."

Veera then asked her," Mother, what can we do to prevent this?"

The lady replied," Only you can prevent it. For that you have to sacrifice your son in the Durga temple here."

Without a moment of Hesitation Veera went to his house and explained the situation. Without any hesitation his wife told, "What is preventing you? The life of our master is more important to us than our son."

Later they woke up their son and told him about what is happening, . The son did not even think a minute and accompanied his father to the Durga Temple. Veera's wife and daughter followed them. The king was watching all this, Veera reached the temple and cut off the head of his son Surya in front o f the deity. A voice was heard from the temple, "Veera, now your master's life is safe."

But Kavya was not able to tolerate her brother's death. So she sacrificed herself before the deity. Dharma seeing that both her children were no more, died there on the spot. Seeing all this Veera also sacrificed himself.

The king who was seeing all this felt sad and wanted to cut off his head also. When he was preparing for that, The Goddess appeared before him and gave life to Veera and all his family members.

Vetala asked Vikrama, "Whose sacrifice is greatest?"

Vikramadhithya told the Vetala, "Of course, it is the sacrifice of the king. It is the job of the Guard and citizen to sacrifice himself for the king. But it is not the duty of the king."

Vetala immediately disengaged itself and went back to the Drumstick tree.

Eighth story of the Vetala:-

Again Vikramadhithya caught hold of the Vetala from the Drumstick tree and started walking towards the house of the sage. The Vetala told its eighth story.

In the eastern shore there was a great town called Thamralipthi. This was ruled by a great king called Chanda Simha.

One day a valorous man called Sathya Sheela who belonged to the royal race reached Thamralipthi. He was very poor. He could not get any job in the palace. But he was offered the job of Kaarpadiga. In this job, one has to work but would not be paid any wages. Sathya sheela took up this job. But since he was not getting any wages, daily he used to collect some goose berries from the forest and tie in the corner of his dress. Whenever he felt hungry, he would quench his hunger by eating these goose berries. Life went on for ten years like this.

One day Chanda Simha went for hunting in the forest. Sathya Sheela was one of those servants accompanying him on feet. During hunting King Chanda Simha started following a wild pig which ran very fast. The king who was riding on a horse back chased him. Sathya Sheela ran behind them. All the followers of the king were left behind. At last Chanda Simha killed the wild pig. Then he saw that he was very tired and had lost his way.

The only one accompanying him was the Kaarpadiga. The king asked his servant, "do you know the way back?" Sathya sheela replied" Yes, king, I know it. But since the sun is very hot we would not be able to travel back now. We would go back in the evening.". The king agreed but told Sathya Sheela, " I am very hungry as well as thirsty. Suppose I do not take any food now or drink some water, I will die." Immediately Sathya Sheela climbed on a tall tree , located a river and brought water from the river. He also gave him , the goose berries. By eating the goose berries and drinking the water, the king became very much refreshed. Then he asked Sathya Sheela, " you seem to be very poor. Are you not getting any wages?". Sathya Sheela replied "King, I am a kaarpadiga and do not get any wages." . After returning back, the king Made Sathya sheela as his commander and body guard. Sathya Sheela also worked sincerely for the king.

One day the king called Sathya Sheela and told him, " I am interested in marrying the princess of Sri Lanka. You please take a ship along with some priests and go to Sri Lanka and request the king for the hand of the princess for my sake. ". Sathya sheela agreed and started the journey. When the ship was mid way to Sri Lanka, suddenly a big flag pole appeared in the sea. Near it there was a horrible whirl pool. The ship was about to be destroyed. Sathya Sheela jumped inside the whirl pool . He slowly reached a big island. In that island there was a very big Durga temple. Sathya sheela entered the temple and offered prayers to the goddess. Then a very pretty lady accompanied by several maid servants entered the temple. The lady was very pretty. Sathya Sheela wanted to marry her. The lady understood his intention and asked her maid servants to take him to the Garden of luxury. In the middle of the garden there was a pond. Sathya Sheela was requested to take bath in the tank. But when he went in to the tank and took a dip, he suddenly found himself in his town Tahmra Lipthi. He approached the king and told him all that has happened to him. The king told Sathya Sheela." We would again go to the same place. I would help you in marrying the lady.

The king and Sathya Sheela again started the journey. When they reached the middle, the flag post came up. The king and Sathya Sheela jumped in to the whirl pool. They reached the same island and went in to the same Durga temple. Then the lady along with her maid servants came. Seeing the king, the pretty lady wanted to marry him. But the king told her, "Pretty one, It would be better for you if you marry my friend Sathya Sheela." The lady agreed and by jumping in to the pond in the garden of luxury, the king reached back to his palace.

The Vetala asked Vikrama " Sir, Sathya Simha gave the goose berry and saved the king's life. The king made the lady whom Sathya Sheela loved as his wife. Whose sacrifice is greater? If you know the answer and do not tell it, your head will break in to pieces. "

Vikrama replied " The sacrifice of Sathya Simha was ordinary , because as a servant , it was his duty to protect the king. But the king id not have any duty. So the sacrifice of the king is greater."

As soon as he told this the Vetala disengaged itself and went to the Drum Stick tree,

(In another version the Vetals asks, "Both Sathya Sheela and the king jumped in to the whirl pool. Who was more braver?"

Vikrama replied, "Ofcourse Sathya Sheela was braver , because when he jumped he was not knowing what is going to happen to him. In case of the king, he already knew about it.")

The ninth story of Vetala:-

Again Vikramadhithya caught hold of the Vetala from the Drumstick tree and started walking towards the house of the sage. The Vetala told its Ninth story.

In the city of Uvisha pura there lived a princess called Mani mala , who was extremely pretty. She was not very intelligent. Her father decided that she should be given in marriage only to a very wise person. A king called Maniman approached him and requested for her hand, as he had decided to marry only a very pretty girl. Mani mala's father put several tests and found that Maniman was indeed wise. So he gave Mani mala in marriage to him,

One day when Mani maala and Mani man were chatting sweet nothings in their golden cot, a row of ants were passing below the cot. When the soldier ant refused to move beyond the legs of the cot, the king ant asked him, "Why don't you throw way the cot and move?" . Then the soldier ant replied , "Sir the king and his queen are lying on the cot. Suppose I throw the cot away , they would both fall down.". Maniman who knew the language of animals hearing this laughed uproariously. His queen asked, "What was so funny? Why are you laughing?". When the king was about to reply, the king ant told him, "if you tell her, your head will break in to pieces.". Then the king told Mani mala, "Darling, I cannot tell you ,because my head will break in to pieces." Mani mala refused to believe this and started throwing tantrums. The king then told her, "OK, I will tell you. But since I will die immediately,

I will lie on the funeral pyre in the cremation ground and then tell you." Mani mala insisted he should do that. A funeral pyre was set up and the king Maniman, was lying on it. At this time one male goat and female goat were grazing in the cremation ground. The female goat wanted the luscious grass in side the well half full of water to eat and told the male goat, "Darling , get me that grass.".Male goat replied, "Foolish girl, I will die , if I try to get that grass. So I would not do it". The female goat became angry and walked away. The king who was hearing all this, suddenly got up from the funeral pyre and told queen Mani mala, "I simply cannot tell you what you want because I will die."

The Vetala asked . OH Vikrama, who was wiser among the two-The goat or the king? If you know the correct answer and do not tell it your head will break in to pieces."

Vikrama replied, "Ofcourse the goat is wiser because, even at the outset, it was not willing to obey the foolish request by the lady,"

As soon as he told this the Vetala disengaged itself and went to the Drum Stick tree,

[Alternative ninth story of Vetala:-

(Some versions give the following as the ninth story)

Again Vikramadhithya caught hold of the Vetala from the Drumstick tree and started walking towards the house of the sage. The Vetala told its Ninth story.

There was a great king called Veera deva. He did not have any children. So he did Thapas(penance) towards Lord Shiva. Lord Shiva appeared before him and blessed him with a valorous son and a very pretty daughter. After that he had a son called Soora deva and a very pretty daughter called Ananga Rathi. Ananga rathi grew up in to a very pretty princess. Veera deva searched through out the world for a suitable groom. He could not find any. So he told his daughter, "dear daughter, I am not able to find any one suitable to marry you. So I request you to choose some one whom you like." The princess replied "Papa, I do not have any specific dreams regarding this. Please choose any one who is pretty and well versed in any particular aspect of knowledge.". The king was pleased and told all his friend kings about his requirement. On a particular day four youth from South India came to the king.

The first one told, " My name is Panchaputtiga, I daily weave five pieces of exquisite cloth. One cloth, I give it to God , one I give it to charity and one use it for myself. If I marry this princess, I will give her one and the last one I will sell in the market and manage my day to day expenses. So please give the princess in marriage to me."

The second one told ," I am a merchant and people call me Bhashagna. I am an expert in languages and even understand the language of birds and animals. So I can make a living wherever I go."

The third one told, " I am called Gadgadhara. I am a soldier. There is none in the world who can defeat me in sword fight. So please give this girl in marriage to me."

The fourth one told, " I am a Brahmin and My name is Jeevadatha. I am an expert in magical chants. I can even give life to a dead man."

Since all the four of them were equally pretty and seemed to be experts as they claimed, The king and the princess were puzzled. Hey Vikrama, can you help them to take the correct decision."

King Vikramadhithya replied, "Ananga rathi belongs to a king's family. She cannot be given in marriage to a merchant nor to the weaver and nor to the Brahmin as they would not be suitable husband to her. She should definitely choose Gadgadhara."

As soon as he told this the Vetala disengaged itself and went to the Drum Stick tree .]

The tenth story of the Vetala:-

Again Vikramadhithya caught hold of the Vetala from the Drumstick tree and started walking towards the house of the sage. The Vetala told its Tenth story.

In the city of Anangapura there was a great merchant called Arthadatha,. He had a very pretty daughter called Madanasena. Both Madanasna and Arthadatha never told a lie in their life. Madanasena grew up and attained marriageable age. Her elder brother's friend Dharmadatha , who knew and played with her from infancy fell hopelessly in love with her. But he did not have the courage to tell her. After quite some time , he did told her, "Dear Pretty girl, I love you a lot.. If I cannot even spend a night with you, I would prefer to die.". Madanasena replied, "My dear friend, you have proposed too late. My father who never tells a lie has fixed my marriage with another merchant friend of his called SAmudhradatha. Then darmadatha told, "Dear friend, then I will take out my life as I do not want to live without you.". Madanasena told him." I already love Samudhradatha but since you are also my friend I do not want you to die. So After my marriage, I would ask my husband to give me permission to spend my first night with you. This would make you live.". Dharmadatha agreed to this proposal. After marriage when Madanasena and Samudradatha were left alone to spend their first night, Madana sena told all that has happened to her husband and asked his permission to spend her first night with Dharma Datha. Though terribly disappointed , Samudradatha agreed to her request. Fully dressed and decorated with several ornaments, Madanasena went to the house of Dharmadatha. However on her way she was caught hold by a very ferocious robber , on seeing her the robber said that he was not interested in her ornaments but her. Then Madanasena told him about the entire story and requested him to leave her without molesting her. She also promised that on her way back, she would make love to him, before going to her husband. The robber agreed. Madanasena went to Darmadutta's house. On seeing her Darmadatta was shocked . He asked her about that night's happenings. She also told him how her husband has given her permission and how a ferocious robber stopped her on the way and how she has promised to spend some part of the night with him on her way back. Dharmdutta was aghast. He feel t her feet and asked her to pardon his lust. He promised her that he would never ever behave badly with any other girl. So Madanasena returned unharmed and met the robber on the way and agreed to spend some time with him. The robber also asked as to what happened. She narrated all the details. The robber fell at her feet and craved her pardon and asked her to go back to her husband. At that time Madanasena offered all her ornaments. But the robber told her, "mother , how can I take them. Seeing how good a person you are , I have decided to leave robbery and become a good man. Madanasena went back to her husband and told him everything. He became happy to know how her action has reformed and accepted her as his.

Then Vetala asked Vikramadhithya, "Whose behaviour and sacrifice was great among these three people?"

Vikramadhithya replied, " Ofcourse that of the robber because the other two were noble people brought up with respect and respectability. So such a behaviour was expected out of them. But in case of the robber, this sort of behaviour was not expected."

As soon as he told this the Vetala disengaged itself and went to the Drum Stick tree

The eleventh story of the Vetala:-

Again Vikramadhithya caught hold of the Vetala from the Drumstick tree and started walking towards the house of the sage. The Vetala told its eleventh story.

Long ago in the town of Villi there was a king called Dharmadwaja.. He had three queens viz Tharavali, Indulekha and Chandana. They were all very pretty and had a very delicate constitution. At times the king used to wonder which of them had the most delicate constitution.

During the spring festival , the king took all the queens to his garden and was engaged in playing with them. At that time the king caught hold of the braided hair of Tharavali. The lotus she was wearing fell on her body, Unable to bear the weight of the flower , she collapsed.. By that time it became night It was a full moon day. The king went for a walk in the terrace along with his second wife Indulekha. As soon as moon light fell on her skin, it started burning and itching. Doctors were summoned immediately. They made her lie down on a bed of lotus leaves and applied sandal paste. Hearing about this the third queen Chandana came out of her palace. She then heard a sound of rice being pounded far away. Her entire body became black because of this.

Dharmadwaja started wondering who was the most delicate and tender among them.

Vetala asked Vikramadhithya, "King , can you help Dharmadwaja? If you know the answer and tell a lie, your head will break in to pieces."

Vikrama replied, "Ofcourse , it is the third queen Chandana. In the other two cases there was some contact with the object . In case of first queen, the flower fell on her. In case of the second queen moon light fell on her. But in case of the third queen, there was no contact . So she is the most delicate."

As soon as he told this the Vetala disengaged itself and went to the Drum Stick tree

The twelfth story of the Vetala:-

Again Vikramadhithya caught hold of the Vetala from the Drumstick tree and started walking towards the house of the sage. The Vetala told its twelfth story.

There was a king called Yasakethu in the Anga country.. He had a very great and responsible minister called Deergadarsi. He had also a very pretty wife called Chandravadana. The king was passionately in love with his wife. He wanted to spend all the day's twenty four hours with her. So he asked his minister Deergadarsi to look after all the administration of the country. In general people started gossiping that Deergadarsi was after power and had made the king slave to love making with his wife. When Deergadarsi heard this rumour he was shocked. That day he consulted his wife Medhavathi about it. She told him, "This is inevitable. I think you ought to go to a long pilgrimage , so that king will not have any other option but to look after the administration of the country. The people of the country then will also realize that you are not interested in the kingship." Deergadarsi thought , this was a great idea. Next day , he told the king, " Great king, I have been told by astrologers that I should go on a long pilgrimage. I am starting tomorrow. So kindly look after the administration. ". The king tried his best to dissuade Deergadarsi from going on a pilgrimage. When he did not agree, he left in a huff.

Next day Deergadarsi left on a pilgrimage without telling any body. His wife did not join him in his pilgrimage. After spending several days, Deergadarsi reached a town which was a port. A businessman of the town took great liking for Deergadarsi.. He took him home and provided him with all comforts. After a few days , the businessman was going to the island of Sumathra for business. Deergadarsi also joined him. While they were returning, suddenly the entire sea started boiling over. From the sea arose a tree made of nine gems. On the top of the tree was sitting a very beautiful maiden with a lyre. She was singing very sad songs about the inevitability of fate. After some time she disappeared in to the sea.

After this Deergadarsi returned to his own town. He then met the king, who was very glad to see him. The king was curious and asked him about all that happened to him. Deergadarsi told him in detail . He also told him about his journey in to the sea and how they met the sad maiden . As soon as he heard about the pretty maiden, the king wanted to see her. He entrusted the entire job of ruling the country to Deergadarsi and started his journey. On the way he met a sage called Kusanabha. The sage told him, that he will meet the pretty lady and marry her. He also told him to travel in the ship of Lakshmidatha, a well known merchant. The king dressed himself as a sage and approached Lakshmidatha. He readily agreed to take him to the journey of the Sumathra island. On their way back , again the tree made of gems came up. They also saw the very pretty maiden singing sad songs. The tree , suddenly disappeared. The king jumped in to the sea. Seeing a sage jump in to the sea Lakshmidatha was upset and was about to commit suicide. Then he he ard a divine voice which assured him of the safety of the king.

The king who jumped in to the sea reached a very pretty town inside the sea.He saw a palace made of Gold. The pillars and windows of the palace were made of gems. When he entered the palace, he saw the pretty lady of the tree , there. .He immediately fell in love with that lady. That lady thinking he was a sage immediately fell at his feet. She asked him, "Who are you? Why have you come to this town under the sea? Though you are dressed like a sage, you are definitely a king."Then the king explained all about himself Then he asked about her. She said, "I am a Vidhyadhara princess called Mrungavathi. For some reason, my father left me alone in this place and has gone somewhere else. Since I live alone, I feel sad . Once in a while I come out of the sea to see others"

The king requested her to marry him. She agreed but told, "During Ashtami and Chathurthi days, I would go alone somewhere. You should neither enquire where I am going nor follow me.,". The king agreed to this condition .They started living a very lovely life there. But when she went somewhere alone after taking his leave on a Chathurthi day, the king followed her in stealth. She went to another island. There an ogre called Jaladushta came and swallowed her. The king was upset, jumped on the ogre and tore his stomach. Mrungawathi came out unscathed. She then told him, "That was due to the curse of my father. On one Chathurthi day, I starved and came to this spot to do pooja to Lord Shiva. My father who is used to take food with me did not get food on that day. . He became furious and cursed me that on all Chathurthi and Ashtami days, this ogre called Jaladushta would swallow me. Then I would come out tearing his stomach. On the day when some king helps me to come out, I can again go to the land of Vidhyadharas. So king, I would be now flying to my land. I was extremely happy with you. "

The king begged her to be with him till he reaches his own native kingdom. Mrungawathi agreed. But due to the passage of time, she lost the power of Vidhyadharas. They reached the town of the king. Minister Deergadarsi received them. But next day, the minister committed suicide.

The Vetala asked, "King , why did Deergadarsi commit suicide.? If you know the correct answer and do not tell it to me, your head will break in to pieces.".

Vikramadhithya replied, "Deergadarsi loved his country. He knew that the king did not take any interest in ruling because he was hopelessly in love with the former queen. Due to him, now the king had brought home a more prettier queen. This would mean, he would not take any interest in ruling the country. He felt that this was because of him. Due to this guilt , he committed suicide."

As soon as he told this the Vetala disengaged itself and went to the Drum Stick tree

The thirteenth story of the Vetala:-
Again Vikramadhithya caught hold of the Vetala from the Drumstick tree and started walking towards the house of the sage. The Vetala told its thirteenth story.
In the town of Ujjaini, there lived a very learned Brahmin called Deva swami. He had an equally learned son called Chandra Swami. Chandra Swami was very much attached to Gambling. One day he went to the Gambling hall and lost al that he had. When he was not able to play his gambling debts, the owners of the gambling joint beat him. At one stage they thought he was dead. So they abandoned him in a forest and went away. After three days Chandra Swami woke up.. He crawled in to a Shiva temple near by. At night one Sanyasi came back with food he has begged from others. He took pity on Chandra Swami and offered him his alms. Then Chandra Swami told him, " Though I am in this pitiable state , I am a learned Brahmin. Since the food that you have is alms, I should not accept it. Then that Sanyasi did some chants. Immediately a golden palace with lot of servants appeared. Some ladies came out of the house and offered food to Chandra Swami. The food was very tasty and the ladies very pretty. Chandra Swami accepted their hospitality that night and slept with them. But when he became morning, he was back in the dilapidated Shiva temple along with the beggar Sanyasi.
Chandra Swami , then begged the Sanyasi to teach him those chants. The Sanyasi told him, "It is extremely difficult to learn those chants. Once I teach you with full concentration , standing in a neck deep water you have to keep on chanting. You would be offered with several goodies by evil spirits, when you are doing the chants If in between you listen to them , the chants would not be effective for you as well as me I would warn you at that time. Then a big funeral pyre will appear before you. You have to jump in to the fire, Then the God will give you the power of the chant.." Chandra Swami insisted that he would do the chants with concentration. When he started chanting , he saw in his reverie, him getting married and getting a child. At this time he was happy and wanted to end it all. The Sanyasi warned him at this juncture. Then the fire appeared before him. His wife and child in the reverie prevented him from jumping in the fire. He was tempted to continue

living with them .Anyway with this doubt he jumped in the fire. Everything disappeared. The Sanyasi also lost the power of the chant.

Vetala asked "Oh king, why did Chandra Swami loose the power of the chant?.If you know the answer and do not tell me the truth, your head will break in to pieces."

Vikrama replied, "Oh Vetala, all meditations should be done with single mindedness and without any doubt. Chandra Swami was attracted by the family life in the reverie and doubt arose in his mind about the need for jumping in the fire. That is why he did not succeed.

As soon as he told this the Vetala disengaged itself and went to the Drum Stick tree

The fourteenth story of the Vetala:-

Again Vikramadhithya caught hold of the Vetala from the Drumstick tree and started walking towards the house of the sage. The Vetala told its fourteenth story.

In the city of Vishala there was a rich merchant called Arthadatha. He was extremely rich. He had an extremely pretty daughter called Anangamanjari. During her child hood she was very close friend of a Brahmin youth called Kamalakara. When she was in teens this turned to love. Kamalakara was very poor and could never even dream of marrying Anangamanjari. Her father searched all over the world for a suitable groom for her and gave her in marriage to a handsome merchant youth called Maniverma. Since Arthadatha could not even imagine living away from his daughter, he made Manivarma live along with them in their house. Manivarma loved Anangamanjari totally. Once he decided to visit his parents for one month. At that time Anangamanjari thought of her lover Kamalakara and became love lorn. One day coming out of her house , she went in to a dense garden and attempted to hang herself. Her friend Malathi found and saved her. When Malathi asked her the reason for such a step, Anangamanjari told to her about her love to Kamalakara. Malathi that day went in search of Kamalakara. She was surprised to find that he was also love lorn and wanted to be with Anangamanjari. Malathi fixed a rendezvous for them in the king's garden. Anangamanjari went to the garden at the appointed time. Kamalakara also came there and he embraced Anangamanjari. Due to the high emotions Anangamanjari died by stoppage of breath. Kamalakara seeing this also died immediately. At this time Maniverma chanced to return. As soon as he saw the dead Anangamanjari , he also died suddenly.

Malathi felt very guilty and she prayed in the temple of Goddess located in the garden. The goddess gave back their lives but without the previous emotions of love. Anangamanjari and Maniverma returned to their home.

Vetala then asked, "Here are three people who died because of love. Whose death is the most strange? If you know the answer and do not tell it, your head will break in to pieces,"

Vikrama replied "the death of Manivarma is most strange. The other two people loved each other and died because of that. But Manivarma died in spite of knowing that her wife died because of the love to another man."

As soon as he told this the Vetala disengaged itself and went to the Drum Stick tree

The fifteenth story of the Vetala:-

Again Vikramadhithya caught hold of the Vetala from the Drumstick tree and started walking towards the house of the sage. The Vetala told its fifteenth story.

There was a poor Brahmin called Vishnu Swami in Pataliputhra. He was very poor. He had four sons. Vishnu swami died suddenly. His four sons had no other go , except learning some trade and earning money. They fixed a spot where they have to return after one year and one traveled towards east, another towards west, another towards south and the other towards north. Exactly after one year they reached the pre determined spot.

The eldest told,"I have learned the art of creating a skeleton even , if I get a piece of bone of the dead person.

The second one told "If I Get the skeleton, I can remake the flesh and skin."

The third one told, "If you get me an animal with flesh, bones and skin, I can create all its internal organs.,"

The fourth one told, "If you give such a recreated animal to me, I can give life to it."

The four brothers wanted to try out , what they have learnt. They went to the nearest forest. They got a piece of bone. The eldest created the skeleton, the second one, flesh and skin and third one the internal organs. Then they saw that it was a lion. The fourth one gave it life. That lion immediately ate all the four brothers.

The Vetala asked , "Who is the guilty among the four, who was responsible for their death?"

Vikrama replied, "Ofcourse, it is the fourth one. Till he gave life to the animal, very well knowing it is a lion, it could not have harmed them."

As soon as he told this the Vetala disengaged itself and went to the Drum Stick tree

The sixteenth story of the Vetala:-

Again Vikramadhithya caught hold of the Vetala from the Drumstick tree and started walking towards the house of the sage. The Vetala told its sixteenth story.

In the town of Varanasi , there was a rich Brahmin called Hari Swami . He had an extremely pretty wife. . One summer day when Hari Swami and his wife were sleeping on a terrace, a Vidhyadhara called Madana Vega saw Hariswami's wife , fell in love with her and took her away. Next day When Hari Swami woke up he thought that his wife has either deserted him or has been kidnapped by some body . Since she was having great love towards him , he thought that she had only been kidnapped. So he decided to go in search of her in all temple towns of India, as she was very religious. He gave away all his property and then started on a pilgrimage. After some time a very horrendous famine made its appearance. Hari Swami could not get any food and was starving. One day he reached a house of another Brahmin, who was giving free food to all., When Hariswami went to his house, the Brahmin's wife gave him sumptuous food in a metal plate., Taking this Hari swami went near a river , kept it on the shore below a huge banyan tree and went to take bath., At that time an eagle caught hold of a poisonous cobra, and was eating it sitting on one of the branches of the great banyan tree. The poison of the cobra fell on the plate kept by Hari Swami. Hari Swami came and ate all the food. Immediately he realized that he has eaten poisonous food. He ran to the Brahmin's house and asked him to summon a doctor and save him, for otherwise the sin of killing a Brahmin(Brahmahathi) would fall on them. But they could not save Hariswami. That Brahmin drove away his wife for supplying poisonous food to Hari Swami.

The Vetala asked ? Whom will the sin of Brahma Hathi affect-The eagle, the snake or the Brahmin couple who gave food?

Vikrama replied , " None of them have committed that sin. The snake did not do any sin , because it spit the poison when its enemy the eagle was eating it. The Sin was not committed by the eagle because it was only taking its normal food. The Brahmin couple had given Hariswami good food and not poisoned food. So they have also not committed any sin.

As soon as he told this the Vetala disengaged itself and went to the Drum Stick tree.

The seventeenth story

Again Vikramadhithya caught hold of the Vetala from the Drumstick tree and started walking towards the house of the sage. The Vetala told its seventeenth story.

In the town of Ayodhya there was king called Veerakethu. There was also a very rich merchant called Rathnadatha. He had an extremely pretty daughter called Rathnavathi. When Rathnavathi came to age, several kings and rich people wanted to marry her. But she rejected their proposal Due to this her father Rathnadatha started getting very worried.

During this time there were a series of Robberies from the homes of rich people in Ayodhya, When the people went and complained to their king Veerakethu, he assured them that he would catch the thief. That night , Veera Kethu dressed himself as a thief and started going round his town. Soon he saw another thief also walking around the town. Both of them got introduced with each other. The real thief invited the king to his house for supper. The king was taken to the deep forest and a Sunken palace there. The real thief asked the king to wait for him and went to take bath. The maid of the thief warned him that he would be killed soon. The king ran away to his palace. Next day he marched with a big army and after a very great war caught the thief. Many of the soldiers of the king were killed. Next day the king decided to hang to death the thief. While the thief was being taken to the place of his death , Rathnavathi saw the thief and fell in love with him. She went to her father and requested him to get her married to the thief. Rathnadatha approached the king and told about the request of his daughter and offered to give away to the country all his property if the king releases the thief. The king refused.

Rathnavathi decided to die by jumping in the burning fire as soon as the thief was hanged. While he was being hanged the thief was told about this. He cried instantly and after some time started laughing, Eventually he died. When Rathnavathi jumped in to the fire . Lord Shiva who was there was impressed by Rathnavathi's love and requested her spirit to ask for one boon. She said, "My father does not have any other children except me. Please bless him with hundred sons." Lord Shiva gave this boon and requested to her to ask another boon. She said, "God make me and the thief alive. Let the thief become a good and individual. Please make him marry me.". Lord Shiva , granted that boon also. Rathnavathi and thief came back to life and married each other.

The Vetala asked Vikrama, "Why did the thief cry first and then laugh?" If you know the correct answer and do not tell it, your head would break in to pieces."

Vikrama told ,"The thief cried because he was not able to properly compensate the great efforts taken by Rathnadatha to save him and he laughed because Rathnavathi who has refused to marry even kings had fallen in love with him."

As soon as he told this the Vetala disengaged itself and went to the Drum Stick tree

The eighteenth story

Again Vikramadhithya caught hold of the Vetala from the Drumstick tree and started walking towards the house of the sage. The Vetala told its Eighteenth story.

Yasakethu was the king of a country called Shiva Pura.He had a very pretty daughter called Sasiprabha ,One day Sasi Prabha along with her friends, had gone to see a temple festival. A Brahmin lad called Manaswamy happened to see her . It was a love at sight mutually. At that time a elephant started running towards Sasi Prabha. Manaswami, rushed near and carried her to safety. Then Sasiprabha went to her home.

Manaswamy was not able to forget Sasi Prabha. So he approached a very learned magician called Moola deva for help. Moola deva promised to help him. He put a magic tablet in his mouth and he became a very old man. He gave another tablet to Manaswami and he became a very pretty girl. Moola deva took the girl Manaswami to the king and spoke thus, "This girl is my would be daughter in law and I have brought her from Benares. But when I came back I found that my son was missing. Now I have to search and find him out. I have a humble request. Please keep this girl in your palace.".The king agreed and entrusted the Manaswamy girl to the princess Sasi Prabha. Soon they became very close friends. One day Sasi Prabha told the Mana Swami girl about her love to Mana Swami. Then Mana

Swami revealed himself by taking out the tablet in his mouth..That day itself they got married with each other in Gandharva tradition and started living with each other. During day Moola Swamy was a girl and night he became himself.

At this time the son of the Chief minister of Shiva pura got married. Sasi Prabha and the Mana Sawmi girl went to attend the marriage. Though he was marrying another girl, the son of the minister fell in love with Mana Swami girl. He told his father that he would commit suicide if he is not allowed to marry Mana swami girl also. Becoming very sad the chief minister requested the king for the hand of Mana Swami girl. The king was not willing as Mana swami girl was entrusted for safe keeping by Moola deva. But the learned people who knew that if the chief minister goes away the country would go to dogs, compelled the king to give Mana swami girl in marriage to the son of the chief minister. Mana swami when asked by the king agreed provided , the son of the minister should after the marriage immediately go on a pilgrimage for six months. The son of the minister agreed. After the marriage when the son of the minister had gone away , Mana swami started living with his other wife.

Meanwhile Moola deva came to know of this. He came along with his son to the king and requested for Mana Swami girl. When the king told the truth Moola deva threatened that he will curse the king and his kingdom. Afraid of this the king gave Sasiprabha in marriage to Moola devas son.

As soon as this was known, Mana swami came back and claimed with the king that he was already married to Sasiprabha in the gandharwa tradition

The Vetala asked"Who is the legal husband of SasiPrabha?.If you know the answer and do not tell it, your head will break in to thousand pieces."

Vikrama told " The leagal husband is the son of Moola Deva as she had been given in marriage following religious traditions for a thief does not have the right to the property stolen by him.."

As soon as he told this the Vetala disengaged itself and went to the Drum Stick tree

Nineteenth story

Again Vikramadhithya caught hold of the Vetala from the Drumstick tree and started walking towards the house of the sage. The Vetala told its Nineteenth story.

There was a great Vidhyadhara king called Jeemootha Kethu. He was bequeathed a Karpaga Vruksha(wish fulfilling tree) . So he lived very happily getting all that he wanted by asking the tree. A son called Jeemootha vahana was born to him (he as a bodhi Sathwa an incarnation of Budha). When Jeemootha vahana became a lad his father entrusted him with the Karpaga tree. Jeemootha Vahana asked permission to do as he wishes with the Karpaga tree. The king agreed. Jeemootha vahana requested the Karpaga tree to give food and wealth for every one in the world and go to heaven. The tree did this and there were no wants for any one in the world. But the cousins of Jeemootha Vahana who did not like what he did waged a war against Jeemootha Kethu, Jeemootha Vahana advised his father to give away the kingship to his cousins .Jeemootha Vahana and his parents went in to the forest and started living there.

In that forest he stuck friendship with a prince called Mithra vasu. One day without knowing who she he is, Jeemootha Vahana feell in love with Malayavathi, the sister of Mithra vasu. With the intervention of Mithra vasu they got married and started living happily.

After the marriage the princess started living with Jeemootha Vahana in the forest. Daily Jeemootha Vahana and his friend used to go for trekking. Once they went for trekking by the sea beach and saw a mountain of bones. When Jeemootha vahana enquired about it Mithra vasu told, " The God Garuda was once fooled by the snakes who were his mother's sisters' children. This made them his sworn enemies. So in spite of the snakes hiding themselves in the Patala(nether world), Garuda , started to hunt and eat as many of them as possible. Due to this Vasuki , the king of snakes approached Garuda and agreed to send one snake per day as his food. These are the skeletons of the snake eaten by Garuda. Even today he must be coming to eat a snake,"\

This made Jeemootha Vahana very sad and he sent back his friend and brother in law Mithra vasu on an errand . While he was waiting he spotted a crying old woman and her son Sanga Chooda. When enquired , the old woman told Jeemootha Vahana , that Sanga Chooda was her only son was the food to be offered to Garuda that day. Jeemootha Vahana offered himself to go instead of Sanga Chooda. Sanga chooda did not agree . He went to bid final farewell to his mother. At that time Garuda came. Jeemootha Vahana offered himself as food. Garuda without realizing that he was not a serpent.

Carried him to the mountain to top so that he can eat him. On the way the gem that jeemootha Vahana was wearing fell at the feet of his wife Malayavathi. She realized that her husband was being eaten by Garuda. Malayavathi along with her brother and the parents of Jeemootha Vahana started following Garuda's path. Sanga Chooda , who came to know of this also started following the path of Garuda.

When Garuda started eating Jeemootha vahana, he found him to be smiling and happy. He felt that something was wrong. At that time Sanga Chooda reached there and told Garuda, that he was a serpent and his food for that day and not Jeemootha Vahana and offered himself. Garuda realized his mistake and asked Jeemootha Vahana to request for any boon. Jeemootha Vahana asked him , "Sir , please stop eating the snakes of Patala from today and give back the life to all these snakes whom you have eaten." Garuda happily agreed and made Jeemootha Vahana the Vidhyadhara king.

Vetala asked, "Whose sacrifice in this story is great? Is it that of Jeemootha Vahana or Sanga Chooda?"

Vikrama replied, "ofcourse the sacrifice of Sanga Chooda is great . Jeemootha Vahana is an incarnation of God and had remarkably kind mind. But Sanga Chooda was an ordinary snake who got back his life. There was no need for him to chase Garuda and offer himself as food.,"

As soon as he told this the Vetala disengaged itself and went to the Drum Stick tree

Twentieth story

Again Vikramadhithya caught hold of the Vetala from the Drumstick tree and started walking towards the house of the sage. The Vetala told its twentieth story.

There was a king called Yasodara in a country called Kanakapura. There was a rich merchant , who had a daughter who was called bewitcher. The merchant approached the king and told him, " I have an exceedingly pretty daughter called Bewitcher. I want to offer her in marriage to you." The king sent some wise men to see that girl to find out whether she has ill omens. When the wise men saw her stunning beauty, they concluded that if their king married her, then he will forget the country and would always be with her. They told a lie that she had some ill omens and asked the king to get her married to their commander in chief.

The girl bewitcher was jilted and became angry at this. So one day she purposefully stood in the way of the king's procession. As soon as the king saw her he fell deeply in love with her. But he could not fulfill his wishes as she was the wife of his commander in chief. Slowly he started loosing his health and was always moody. His valet guessed the reason for this and informed the ministers of the king. They in turn told the king that the girl bewitcher was his subject and he could make her his wife at any time. But the just king did not agree to this. Hearing about this the commander in chief again and again offered his wife as gift to the king. Slowly the king died. Unable to bear the sorrow the Commander in chief committed suicide. The Vetala asked, "Who is a better person, the king or the commander in chief?"

Vikrama replied "Ofcourse the king, because though he could have easily accepted the girl, he did not do it due to his high regard for principles. What the commander in chief did was the duty of a servant."

As soon as he told this the Vetala disengaged itself and went to the Drum Stick tree

Twenty first story

Again Vikramadhithya caught hold of the Vetala from the Drumstick tree and started walking towards the house of the sage. The Vetala told its twenty first story.

There was a king called Chandravaloka in the country called ChithraKoota. One day while hunting he lost his way and reached the hermitage of Sage Kanva. There he met a girl called Indraprabha , who was extremely pretty. With in an instant both of them fell in love with each other and wanted to get married. That day Chandravaloka approached sage Kanva and made a request for the hand of Indraprabha., The saint readily agreed. The marriage was celebrated next day. After living a week there, the king and his bride left to his capital town of Chithrakoota. On the way , one night they happened to spend below a banyan tree. A Brahma Rakshas who was occupying the tree got very angry with this and was about to kill him. On the request of Indra Prabha, that Brahma Rakshas left them with a condition that they should offer in sacrifice a young Brahmin boy , who was willingly prepared to be sacrificed .Not only that, while he was being sacrificed, his mother hold his feet and the father should hold his hands. The king Chadravaloka should do the act of cutting his head and offering it to the Goddess below the tree. If this was not done within a week, The Brahma Rakshas threatened that he would gobble up them both, in whichever place they hid themselves.

Greatly scared the king and his wife reached Chithrakoota. They confessed their problem to the elderly prime minister of the country. He sent round a notice to all the people that one ton of gold would be offered to the family of the Brahmin boy who would agree to this condition. One Brahmin boy brought it to the notice of his very poor parents and suggested to them that he would offer himself for the sacrifice. Due to the great money that they would get the parents also agreed. The king went along with the boy and , his mother held his feet and father his hands and Chandravaloka was about to cut off his head. At that time the Brahmin boy laughed very loudly. All the people assemble there saluted that boy.

The Vetala asked, "Why did the Brahmin boy laugh?" If you know the correct answer and do not tell it , your head would break in to pieces.

King Vikrama replied" When any person gets into trouble any person will approach their parents for help. If they are not able to help, they would approach the king. When king was not able to help , they would approach the God.

In this case, his parents were helping in the sacrifice, the king was sacrificing him for the sake of the God. Thinking about ths the Brahmin boy laughed.

As soon as he told this the Vetala disengaged itself and went to the Drum Stick tree

Twenty second story.

Again Vikramadhithya caught hold of the Vetala from the Drumstick tree and started walking towards the house of the sage. The Vetala told its twenty second story.

Lot of learned Brahmins were living in city called Somavathi in the Kalinga country. Among them one of the greatest was Yagna soma. After a long time he did not get any children but at a ripe old age he got a son. He was called

Deva Soma

Deva some grew up in to a very learned lad. Unfortunately he died at the age of sixteen. His parents became very sad and refused to part with the dead body. The learned people of the village consoled him in various ways and Deva Soma's body was taken to the cremation ground. All people accompanying the dead body were crying loudly.

In the cremation ground there lived a very old sage who had mastered the occult powers. He asked his disciple to go and find out the reason for so much sorrow. The disciple refused to go , because he was angry with his teacher. Then the teacher saint himself went there. The body of deva Soma was pretty but that of the saint was worn out by old age. So the saint decided to leave his body and enter the body of Deva Soma. After deciding this he first cried and then he danced with joy. When his soul entered the body of Deva Soma, he woke up from death. The sage within deva soma told them, "In this brief period of death , I have seen God. He wanted me to lead a life of the sage. People including his parents agreed with sorrow and left the cremation ground.

Vetala asked , "Why did the sage cry first and then dance with joy."

King Vikrama replied, "The sage had got used to his body since birth. He had achieved a lot including mastery of the occult using that old body. So he cried because of the sorrow at leaving that body. But then he realized that by entering the body of the youth, he could master the occult further and live a very healthy life.. Because of this knowledge he danced with joy."

As soon as he told this the Vetala disengaged itself and went to the Drum Stick tree

Twenty third story(first version)

Again Vikramadhithya caught hold of the Vetala from the Drumstick tree and started walking towards the house of the sage. The Vetala told its twenty third story

There was a king called Nakshtra Raja in the town of Gopura. One day he happened to see a very pretty girl called Avanthikal in the street. He married her , then and there and was taking her to his native place. Here he was attacked by a gang of thieves. Nakshtra raja killed all of them.. Then he told Avanthikal to take rest under a tree and left to bring some food for both of them. There a prostitute got attracted by him and kept him with herself.

When Avanthikal was getting scared , one merchant who happened to go that way was attracted by her and took her with him. One day while they were alone a mouse disturbed them. The merchant caught and killed the mouse. He bragged about this to Avanthikal. Avanthikal then told about her previous lover who had killed several thieves and not only that but she committed suicide. The merchant thought that the king Nakashtra raja would come and trouble him further. So he also committed suicide. By this time the king returned and he also committed suicide. At that time the prostitute came in search of the king and finding that she was the reason of death of so many people, she also died.

Vetala asked, "whose suicide is the greatest?"

King Vikrama replied., "The death of the prostitute is greatest because she left her life on her principle. In the case of others, they all died due to passion,."

As soon as he told this the Vetala disengaged itself and went to the Drum Stick tree

Twenty third story (second version)

Again Vikramadhithya caught hold of the Vetala from the Drumstick tree and started walking towards the house of the sage. The Vetala told its twenty third story

In the city of Tharalipthi there was a great merchant , His only daughter was Dhanavathi.When she became a lass , the merchant died.. All his relatives stole away all the money of the merchant. Then her mother Hiranyasvathi , took all the money and jewels available and fled from that town with her daughter. When they were walking in darkness through the forest , Hiranyavathi's shoulders hit against the feet of a thief who was hanged to death. He cried in pain. Hiranyavathi said sorry. Then that thief told her that to get salvation he needed a son. So if Hiranyavathi agrees to marry her daughter to him, he would give all his stolen wealth and also permit

Dhanavathi to beget a son from any male of her choice. Hiranyavathi agreed to this proposal and a marriage was performed to the thief. As soon as the marriage was performed , the thief died. After cremating him mother and daughter reached the town of Vakraloka and started living a wealthy life there. One day Dhanavathi saw a very learned Brahmin in the next house and wanted to beget a son through him. His name was Manaswami. He wanted to spent the nights with a prostitute who used to charge five hundred gold coins for a night. So when Hiranyavathi approached him, he agree to be with Dhanavathi for a night , provided he was given 500 gold coins. Hiranayavathi agreed .Manaswami spent one night with Dhanavathi. After 10 months when Dhanavathi was about to beget a child, she had a dream in which God Shiva appeared and told her " A son will be born to you. Take him and abandon him in front of the palace along with one thousand coins." Dhanavathi followed the instructions .

That night God told the king about this child and asked him to bring him up and make him the king of the country. The king who was not having any children, rushed our brought the child along with one thousand coins and brought him up. He called him Chandra Prabhan. The boy grew up in to a very great king. He was made the king after his father's death. To grant salvation to his father Chandra Prabhan went to Benaras and offered Pinda(rice balls) to the fire. But as soon as he offered the rice balls, three hands were extended to receive the Pinda. The hands were that of the thief, Brahmin and the king.

Vetala asked," In which hand should he offer the pinda?" and warned Vikrama that knowing the correct answer if he does not tell it , his head will break in to pieces.

Vikrama replied, "He should offer it to the hand of the thief because, the Brahmin got money to beget him and the king was given money to nurture him. So both of them were only doing the job of a servant and not father."

As soon as he told this the Vetala disengaged itself and went to the Drum Stick tree

The twenty fourth story

Again Vikramadhithya caught hold of the Vetala from the Drumstick tree and started walking towards the house of the sage. The Vetala told its twenty fourth story.

There was king called Dharma. He had a wife called Chandravathi. They had a daughter called Lavanyvathi. Once relatives of Dharma usurped his kingdom and drove the royal family out. Dharma was carrying with him lots of Gold and money. On their way they had to cross a forest full of thieves. Dhrama asked his wife and daughter to flee. Though Dharma fought with the thieves he was soon overpowered and killed. Chandravathi who was watching all this hiding from a distance started fleeing further.

During this time , the king of a nearby town was walking in the same forest along with his son. They both saw footprints of two ladies fleeing. One feet was small and another big. They decided that the father would marry the girl with large feet and the son would marry the lady with small feet.

Then the found out the story of the queen and his daughter. Unfortunately the daughter had a big feet and the mother had a small feet. Sticking to their original decision the father married the daughter and the son married the mother. Eventually both of them gave birth to a son and a daughter.

The Vetala Asked "How many type of relations to the children born to the king and his son have? What is their relation? And warned that Vikrama has to tell the correct answer if he knew it and If he does not tell the correct answer, knowing it , his head will break.

Vikrama was completely puzzled and did not tell any answer but continued to carry the Vetala. Then the Vetala addressed him as King Vikramadhithya and asked his pardon and then told its story.

The story of Vetala

Then Vetala told its own story, "I was a priest of a temple in Chozha desa and was called Kalathiyan., I used to offer lord Shiva several food articles daily as Naivedhyam, . One night having forgot to take the food articles offered to the God back home, I reopened the shut doors of the temple. There I saw Goddess Parvathi lying on the lap of Lord Shiva. He was telling all the stories that I told you just now. I returned home late and when wife became angry I told her about the incident and she compelled me to tell her all the stories. I made her promise not to tell the stories to any one . But she told them to several people . Lord Shiva got very angry at this and cursed me to become a Vetala. When I begged him for forgiveness, he asked me to hang upside down on a drum stick tree in this forest. He told that you would one day come to catch me. He instructed me to tell all those 24 stories. He further said that you will answer the questions at the end of the first 23 stories but would not be able to answer the question at the end of the last story. He further told me to serve you all your life and when You go to heaven, I will also get salvation."

The Vetala then told him, " The sage Gnanaseela who has requested to bring me is not a good man. He wants to become the greatest person and wants me as his slave. As soon as you take me there he would request you to salute falling on the floor , the fire that he is worshipping with an intention of cutting your head and making it fall in the fire. Please tell him that you do not know how to salute falling on the floor. He will show you. Then cut his head off and put in the fire."

Vikrama agreed and acted accordingly. Then Goddess Kali appeared before Vikrama and said, "Son, I am happy with you. Request for the boons that you want."

Vikrama said, "This slave of yours should always have a pure mind and great power and you should come before me, whenever I request. Not only that the 999 kings who have been sacrificed by Gnanaseela should be given their life back." Goddess Kali gave those boons and disappeared.

Vikrama then returned to his capital along with Vetala who became his slave.

www.ingramcontent.com/pod-product-compliance
Lightning Source LLC
Chambersburg PA
CBHW031516150726
47990CB00007B/3044